The
Last
Little
Cat

By

Meindert DeJong

Pictures by

Jim McMullan

The Last Little Cat

Whole Spirit Press

1905 S. Clarkson St.

Denver, Colorado 80210

http://wholespiritpress.com

sales@wholespiritpress.com

ISBN Number: 978-1-892857-00-2

WHOLE SPIRIT PRESS

1905 S. Clarkson St.
Denver, Colorado 80210
Toll Free: 1-877-488-3774
Internet: http://wholespiritpress.com
Email: sales@wholespiritpress.com

Whole Spirit Press is committed to publishing books that have true value in the lives of our youth. We specialize in renewing out-of-print books that help the reader learn from the inside out.

We focus our publishing efforts on quality fairy tales, fantasy, history, legend, and love. Our primary markets are private and home-schools around the world.

Please contact us with your suggestions for meaningful out-of-print books that you feel should once again be available.

For Mohammed, my cat.

For Mohammed came to me.

BELIEVE IT! It would seem that the last little cat was born in the last place a cat should be born—even a last little cat. The little black kitten was born in a kennel! And it was the last kitten of a whole litter of kittens—six kittens had been born, after that the last little cat still was born. Born in a nest—mind you—in a chicken nest in a barn that was now a dog kennel.

The barn had once been a chicken barn, but now it was full of dogs and dog cages, and dog noises and dog din. Up from the floor of the barn rose the cages—rows and rows of cages, cages above cages—floor-low and man-high.

And in each and every cage—floor-low, man-high—was a barking dog.

There were dogs in all the cages—all kinds of dogs. But all of them were barking dogs. There were no quiet dogs. Not in any of the cages—floor-low, man-high—any quiet dogs.

Except one!

This one quiet dog was in a cage set on top of the row of cages against the end wall of the barn. Set on top of the other cages this way, this dog's cage was higher than man-high, and almost higher than a man could reach. The dog was there in a cage set by itself because he belonged to the man who owned the kennel-barn. The dog was blind!

He was the kennel-man's own dog. He was so old that he was blind and stiff. He was so old that he was almost

deaf, and he could smell but little. But he could feel! He could feel hunger and thirst, and warmth and cold, and love and kindness, and loneliness and longing. He could still feel all that! And he was quiet. He was so old that he was blind and quiet.

It could be seen that the barn that was now full of dogs and dog noises and din had once been a chicken barn. Against the end wall of the barn there still were chicken nests, row upon row of cubbyhole chicken nests, one above the other. But now they weren't chicken nests with straw in them, and eggs in them, and chickens laying eggs in them—now they were just empty cubbyholes to put things in for dogs.

But the highest row of cubbyhole nests was higher than man-high, and higher than a man could reach. It was even higher than the high cage of the old blind dog. This top row of chicken nests had not been cleaned of straw and filled with things for dogs. And in the straw of one of those nests—where chickens once had laid their eggs—the mother cat had put her young. Her whole litter of six kittens! And then still the last little black kitten!

It was a strange place for a mother cat to have her kittens—in a chicken nest in a kennel full of dogs! But there was no other secret, hidden, unseen place for this mother cat to have her young. She belonged in the kennel-barn. She lived there! She was kept there to keep down the rats and the mice that stole the food for the dogs— so it was there that she had to have her kittens. And no other place!

The high cubbyhole chicken nest was far too small for a litter of six kittens, and then still the last little

black kitten. Oh, the first nine days, when the kittens still were blind and small, there was room in the nest for them all with the mother. But there was no place for the last little cat for milk from the mother. The six kittens took all the places for milk. There was no place until the other six kittens were done with drinking milk. Then there was a place, but then there was no milk.

The six other kittens drank the milk, and grew and grew. But as *they* grew, the nest grew smaller. Then there was hardly a place in the nest for the last little cat. Always the little cat was at the outermost edge of the nest. It would try to snuggle itself warm against the other kittens, but at the outer edge it would only get half warm. It was always half cold. It was half warm, and half cold, and all hungry. And it needed to be full and warm—full of lovely warm milk, and warm.

On the ninth day came the time for the kittens to open their eyes. In the morning of the ninth day the six kittens opened their eyes. In the late afternoon the last little cat opened its eyes.

When the little cat opened its eyes, it —as always—was at the outermost edge of the nest. Its little head was pushed over the edge. The little cat opened its eyes and looked down at the barking dogs in the barn.

Of course, the little cat did not see all the dogs, or all the long rows of dog cages—it could not see that far with its new eyes. All it really could see was the high cage of the old dog just below the high nest. The old dog did not look up at the last little cat—the old dog was blind. But with its new eyes the last little cat looked down on the old quiet dog.

After the day of the opening of eyes there came another great day. On this day the mother cat took her kittens out of the nest by the scruff of their necks, and—one by one—she carried them down to the floor to get them used to the barking dogs. But when she had carried the sixth kitten down, she did not come back up for the last little cat.

The little cat was too weak and scrawny and wobbly to be out of the nest.

Down on the floor the mother cat put her tail up straight and calm and wise, and led her six kittens through the barn among the cages of the barking dogs—to show and teach her kittens that they need not be afraid of dogs in cages. Then—like their mother—the six kittens put their slim little pencil-tails up straight, and walked in single file behind their mother among the cages of the dogs. And they were not afraid!

The last little cat wanted to join the parade of the six kittens—even if, as the last little cat, it would have to come last with its little pencil-tail up! The little cat scrambled out of the high nest to join in the pencil-tail parade of the kittens.

Just a little while before the parade of the mother cat and the kittens, the man had brought his old dog a bowl of warm milk. Now the last little cat was pulling itself over the edge of the high nest. The old dog—carefully, neatly, because he was blind—was lapping his milk from the white bowl. And then the little cat fell! But the last little cat did not fall all the way to the floor—it fell on the cage of the old blind dog. The old deaf dog did not hear the little cat fall on the wire top of his cage—the old dog went on lapping his lovely warm milk.

On top of the cage the little cat picked itself up, and tried to get down to its mother and the six kittens on the floor. The little cat could not walk on wires! It slipped. It managed to catch itself by its front paws. It managed to hook its thin nails around one of the wires. There it hung from the wire. But the little cat could not hang from a wire! Again the little cat fell.

It fell into the cage of the old blind dog, fell on top of the dog—right on his head! The jar of the little cat's fall on his head made the old dog's whole chin dip into the milk—down to the bottom of the deep white bowl. The old blind dog jerked his chin up out of the milk so hard he tipped the bowl. The milk spilled out into the sawdust on the floor of the cage. And the old dog growled.

The milk was gone, the bowl lay tipped, the little cat lay behind the tipped bowl. The old dog could not see, could hardly hear, could hardly smell, but he reached out over the tipped-over bowl to feel what had happened in his cage. Then over the tipped bowl the old dog touched the little cat with his milk-wet chin.

Immediately the little cat stood up, the little cat reached up, the little cat touched its mouth to the old dog's milk-wet chin. Then the little cat tasted milk—warm milk! The little cat began to scrub the old dog's chin for the lovely taste of the lovely warm milk.

The old dog still could feel! He loved the feel of the rough scrubbing tongue of the little cat. He stretched down to the little cat to be scrubbed still more, still better. With its pencil-tail up, the little cat stood between the stretched paws of the dog, and scrubbed, and scrubbed, and scrubbed his chin.

It soothed the old blind dog—it made him sleepy. Slowly his sleepy chin came down over the little cat between his paws. The little cat tucked itself down in under the dog's woolly chin. And there the little cat found it was warm. They both became warm and sleepy together, and they slept together—there in the cage with the tipped-over bowl.

From that day on the old blind dog and the last little cat lived together, drank their bowl of milk together, slept together. For the first time in its life the last little cat had milk, warm milk, and milk enough. For the first time the little cat was warm, all warm, and warm enough. It loved the milk, it loved the warmth, it loved the old blind dog. And the lonely blind dog loved the little cat. There was love enough for the last little cat in the cage with the old blind dog. And the little cat grew and grew. And the days came, and the days went.

The man came, and the man went. The man owned the kennel-barn, and took care of all the dogs. But busy as he was, the man came twice a day to bring his dog his bowl of milk. He came in the morning, he came in the evening. But morning or evening when the man came and reached up high to slide the bowl of milk into the cage, the old blind dog was mostly asleep. And tucked down in under the dog's woolly chin, the little cat was mostly asleep. The man never saw the little cat in the high cage.

Then a warm, sunshiny day came in spring. This warm day in spring the man came in the afternoon to the high cage, long before the time of the evening bowl of milk. The man reached high, and took down the cage. He carried it away so softly and quietly he never woke the sleeping dog. He never even woke the sleeping cat tucked down in under the old dog's chin. The man never saw the last little cat.

The man carried the cage outside the barn and set the cage in a spot of sun, so that the sun would warm the dog, and warm all the stiffness out of him. Then the man tiptoed away. The old dog slept on in the warming sun, but the sunlight awakened the little cat.

The last little cat peered out from under the old dog's chin, and—THERE WAS THE WORLD.

The little cat had not known about the world. The last little cat had not known there was a world—except the world of barking dogs inside the kennel-barn. HERE WAS THE WORLD.

Here was the world, but the old dog went on sleeping. And in the world was sunshine and song. Songs in the trees, songs in the grass. Oh, many songs and chirpings were coming up from the grassy field that stretched out from the kennel barn. The big field seemed all the world to the little cat.

The last little cat left the sleeping dog, for out there was the world! It squeezed between the wire of the cage, and went out into the world. And the whole world was as warm as a bowlful of milk.

In the sunshiny big field there were insect songs above the grass and in the grass. But the insects couldn't be caught. The big bees rumbled, but wouldn't let themselves be caught by the little cat. A butterfly flew far too high for the little cat's highest, mightiest leaps with outstretched paws stretched high.

But under the deep green grass was the mousy rattle of dry dead grass. And every dry, rattling mouse-tail stalk had

17

to be stalked through the deep grass,
and pounced on, and mauled, and
bitten to shreds.

And all about the little cat, above the
grass and in the grass, were bird song

and insect song. And the sky was big, and the field was big, and the fun was big, and everywhere was sunshine. The world was as warm as a bowl of milk.

Then the sun went down!

The sun went down, the fun was done, the little cat was tired and hungry from all the fun. And the time of the bowlful of warm milk had come.

The kennel-barn rose up from the end of the grassy field—the barn was high, and not hard to find. The little cat went back to the barn, for the time for the bowlful of warm milk had come.

The barn rose high, the barn was not far, but by the time the last little cat had found the barn, and then the door to the kennel-barn, the sun had long gone down.

The little cat had found the door, but there was no cage with a sleeping blind dog at the barn door. The little cat did not know, but when the sun had gone down, and the sun warmth had gone, and the time for the bowlful of warm milk had come, the man had come, and had carried the cage and the old blind dog and the bowlful of milk into the barn.

Now the sun was gone, and the time for the bowlful of milk was gone, and the little cat sat before the closed door. The door was closed and locked for the night, but the last little cat sat before the thick door. The little cat cried. But no one heard the small cries of the cat.

The last little cat sat and cried so long that at last it could cry no more. It still opened its mouth to make a cry, but no sound came to make the cry. And the time of the bowlful of warm milk was long gone. And the time of the lovely long sleep after the milk. And the time of the lovely warm sun.

With the sun gone, the shadows came, and the cold of the evening, and the dark of the night. The world wasn't warm as a bowlful of milk any more. The world had become cold and dark.

The last little cat sat at the door, but it no longer looked up and cried up at the door. It stared and looked into the dark. And the last little cat stood up, and walked toward the dark and the shadows—and wandered away from the barn and the door.

It wandered into the world, but now the world was not full of sunshine and song; now the world was a world of dark night. The little cat went into the world, and the little cat's world was a row of houses, stretching out from the barn in the night. The little cat's world was a world of seven houses with closed doors in the night.

The last little cat went into the world —and the world was a world of closed doors.

The little cat came to the back yard of the first house in the row of seven big houses. At the back of the house the little cat also found a door. The little cat sat and cried before the closed door. It opened its mouth to make the cries, but no sound came to make the cries—and nobody heard, nobody came. Nobody opened the door.

But as if *he* had heard the cries that the last little cat couldn't cry, a big dog came rushing into the yard. The dog saw the cat, and he stopped and stood stiff, and he uttered a stiff, hard bark. The last little cat saw the dog. Up came its stub-of-a-pencil tail—up it came, straight up! And the little cat ran to the dog to snuggle itself between the dog's paws, and tuck itself in under his chin —to sleep with the dog. The big dog growled a stiff growl. The little cat just came on.

It made the dog doubtful. This was no way for a cat to behave—come at a dog! Cats were supposed to scare and run, and scoot up the nearest, tallest tree—for a dog! But this little cat just came on!

The doubtful dog looked this way and that. He twisted this way and that —he just did not know what to do. He stood stiff again, as if to think. But the only thing he could think—was to run himself. He turned tail and ran.

All in a moment the dog was gone, and the little cat stood alone. With its

pencil-tail up, the last little cat stood in the yard, and cried to the dog to come back. But no sound came to make the cry to call the big dog back.

But a sound came out of the next yard! The sound came from beyond the row of trees between the first yard and the second yard. And the sound that came to the little cat's ears was like the sound of the closing of a door—the slow, creaky closing of a door. The last little cat ran toward the sound, and to the door of the second house. But when it came to the back door—the door was tight and thick and shut.

Then the sound came again—the sound of the slow, creaky door. But the sound came from the yard of the second house. And the sound wasn't the sound made by a door—the sound was made by a sleeping dog. The sound was a snore!

Way back in the back yard of the second house there was a small dog kennel. The little kennel had been built to look just like a house. It had a sharp roof like the roof of a house—it even had a chimney. And it had a small door —like the front door of a house. Inside the small open door lay a bulldog sound asleep. The bulldog with his pushed-in nose snored in his sleep. But the little cat with its tail straight up hurried in through the open door to the snoring dog. It crept between the stretched paws of the sleeping dog.

Suddenly the dog felt the crawly, mouse feeling of the last little cat tucking itself in under his chin for a warm sleep. The dog scared awake with a roar. He leaped straight up and out of his kennel, straight up and over the little cat. His chain rattled out behind him past the little cat.

The scared dog could run only as far as the length of his chain, then the chain jerked him back, and threw him down to the ground. There lay the bulldog outside his kennel at the end of his chain. The little cat sat in his kennel. The dog lay miserably on the ground, and looked miserably at the cat in his kennel. And then he yelped for help! He yelped and yelped and yelped for help! And he made miserable sounds through his pushed-in nose.

In the second house they heard the yelps and the bulldog's miserable sounds. The door of the house flew open, and a man came running with a flashlight. He flashed the light into the yard—there lay the dog thrown to the ground at the end of his chain. The man flashed the light into the kennel— there sat a little cat.

"A cat!" the disgusted man said loudly to the bulldog. "And only a small little cat at that! I thought the way you were yelping it was at least a skunk or two—or maybe even three! But one small cat! Why, for punishment I ought to let you stay out on the damp, cold ground all night—and let the cat sleep in your kennel!"

The man got down on hands and knees and put his face before the little door. His big face filled the door. Inside the kennel the little cat stared with big saucer eyes at the big face that filled the door. "You can't stay in there," the big face said to the big-eyed cat. "With you in there that dog of mine would yelp all night. Besides, you shouldn't be in *his* house—you should be in your own house. At night little cats like you should be at home—or they get lost."

He tried to reach the little cat, but
the little cat drew back. "Well, if I can't
pull you out," the big face said, "I'll
have to scare you out! Scat, cat!" And
the man raised up and slapped his
hand down on the roof of the little
kennel-house.

The sound of the slap on the roof was like the sound of a clap of thunder. The little scared cat shot out of the house between the knees of the kneeling man. It tried to hide between the knees. But the man picked up the trembling cat. "Oh, I didn't mean to scare you like that! I only meant to scare you home." He stroked the little cat, and cuddled it in the crook of his arm.

It was warm in the crook of the big man's arm, and the little cat was not afraid any more. The little cat purred for the man. The man picked up the flashlight and flashed the light on the little cat as he held it in the crook of his arm. "Hey," the man said, "now that I can see you better, I think I know where you belong. Why, right next door, little cat! It seems to me I've seen a cat there off and on. Yes, I do believe you live next door, and for scaring you so, I'll carry you home."

The man took the little cat onto the porch and to the back door of the third house. The man pounded on the door. Nobody answered, nobody came.

"That's funny," the man said to the little cat. "I'm sure they're home—the lights are on. It must be that they're looking at television, and didn't hear my knock. But that reminds me! I'm missing my own television program; it's on right now."

He knocked hard and impatiently on the thick, solid door. Nobody answered, nobody came.

The man looked down at the little cat in the crook of his arm. "I'm sure you belong here," he said doubtfully. "I'm sure I've seen a cat here off and on. Well, no doubt after the television program they'll come to the door and let you in. But I'm missing *my* program!" Suddenly he set the little cat down, and suddenly he rushed away home—and left the last little cat sitting before the closed door.

Nobody in the third house came to the door, but the big yellow cat that lived in the third house came home. It saw the little cat on its porch. It flattened itself, and it came so stealthily and sneakingly on its padded sneak feet, the little cat never saw it until it pounced.

In a great scare the little cat spat off the porch. The big cat leaped down from the porch after it. It chased the little cat out of its yard, and into the fourth yard, and up a big tree. The big cat came right up the tree after the last little cat. The little scared cat had to keep climbing and climbing—on and on, and up and up, to the top of the big tree. Still the big yellow cat kept on climbing after it. The little scared cat crawled out on the highest limb in the top of the tree, until at last the limb got so thin it bent down, and swayed, and shivered. That scared the big yellow cat. It backed away into the tree. It backed all the way down the big tree to the ground.

Safe on the ground the big cat stayed under the tree. It yowled wicked warnings up into the tree—for the little cat never to dare to try to come down again. The last little cat clung to the shivering limb.

The voice of the big cat came up from the ground, and the ground was very far down. The little cat looked down into the darkness under the tree, and down, down, down was so very far down, the little cat dug its nails into the bark, and clung to the high, shivering limb. And the voice of the fierce, yowling cat came up from the ground in the darkness.

In the third house that was now next door—even with the television turned on loud—they heard the yowling warnings of the yellow cat. Now they opened the door! The door opened wide and the yellow light shone out of the house for the yellow cat. The cat went in through the bright wide-open door. Then the door closed, and the little cat clung to the limb in the darkness.

Later—much later—in some hour of the night, the silver moon came out. The moon shone down on the top of the tree and the last little cat. The moon made the whole top of the tree light and silver. The little cat looked up at the moon, and the moon was a white milky bowl in the sky, and the last little cat cried a soundless cry up at the white moon.

The little cat cried at the light of the moon that shone in the top of the tree, but it did not dare to go down the high tree, for under the tree was the darkness. The darkness was under the tree, and the darkness was down,

down, and very far down. Then the moon dipped away into the clouds, and then all was darkness.

At last the moon came out of the clouds, and when once again the moon shone, then the little cat dared. By looking up at the moon and the light of the moon, the little cat dared. The little cat let go its cramped hold on the high, shivering limb, and the little cat began to climb down—all the time looking up at the moon. When the moon went away into clouds, the little cat clung wherever it was. But all the while the silver moon shone the little cat dared to climb down—for the moon was a white milky bowl in the sky, and a white friendly light.

Then the moon at last was gone, and did not come to shine again. The morning came. The cold and the dark of the night changed to the cold and the gray of the morning. The last little cat was halfway down the big tree. The little cat rested from all its hard climbing by hanging over a branch on its stomach, halfway up the tree.

In the early gray morning the door of the fourth house opened wide. A woman in pajamas let a fuzzy puppy out, and closed the door. The puppy came on alone into the yard. The puppy came to the tree. The little cat hung with its head down and its little tail down over the branch. But up came its stub-of-a-pencil tail at the sight of the puppy.

The last little cat was so glad to see the puppy it quite forgot it still was halfway up the tree. It wriggled free, and it let itself fall—down to the ground and the puppy. It landed on its four little paws before the surprised little puppy. It touched its nose to the nose

of the puppy. The pleased little puppy
was as delighted with the little cat as
the little cat was with him. He wiggled
and waggled, and they touched noses
again. The puppy slobbered the little
cat with a very wet tongue. The little
cat scrubbed the puppy with its very
rough tongue. And they were friends!

But the door of the fourth house
opened again. The woman in pajamas
sleepily called to her puppy. The puppy
went storming away to the woman. But

right beside the puppy, the last little cat stormed away to the woman. Together they stormed through the door, and into the house over the woman's bare feet. The sleepy woman looked at her feet. Her sleepy eyes became saucer eyes. She opened her mouth as wide as a saucer.

She screamed up the stairs: "John, John, come down! A cat chased our puppy into the house! John, John,

come down. There's a cat in the house!"

A sleepy man came stumbling down the stairs, and grabbed the cat, and opened the door, and dropped the cat outside the door. "Wherever you belong," he rumbled sleepily, "you don't belong in here." He closed the door.

The last little cat sat outside the door, and cried to itself. It opened its mouth to cry to itself, but no sound came to make the cry—not even to itself. And it was early in the morning—long after the moon, and long, long, long before the warm sun. But the cold gray morning was wearing on to the sun! The morning was waiting slowly for the coming of the bright, warm sun. The last little cat did not know. It did not know that the sun came again every day in the morning to warm the world and little cold cats. The little cat sat crying to itself.

The last little cat could not hear itself cry, but it heard another crying—a crying and a calling in a yard two houses away. In the sixth yard two houses away a woman was calling: "Kitty, Kitty, Kitty." She called over and over again—"Kitty, Kitty, Kitty"—in the cold gray morning. The last little cat did not know what Kitty meant, but it was a sound in the lonely morning. The last little cat hurried toward the sound.

The last little cat could not know that the woman in the sixth yard was calling her own big, black, battle-scarred, battle-worn warrior cat that had been out fighting all night long. The little cat did not know that the woman was standing in her back yard with a white bowl that was full of meat to lure her fighting cat home. The little cat did not know—it just went to the calling voice, for it was a sound in the morning.

The little cat did not get to the sixth yard—the yard of the woman with her bowl of meat. The last little cat got only as far as the fifth yard—the yard of the seven early children.

The seven children had got up so early in the slate-gray morning, they'd even got their mother up with all their noise. It was early, but the sun half promised to come out, so the mother bundled up the seven children, and sent them out to play in the yard, where they could be as noisy as they pleased.

The little cat hurried through the fifth yard to get to the kitty-calling woman in the sixth yard. There came seven children in a row out of the door of the fifth house. The last little cat— born in a kennel—had never seen a child before, had never even *heard* a child before. But here came seven shouting children!

The seven children saw the cat. Seven surprised, delighted children came running, squealing, yelling out to the little cat. The little cat scooted under a car in the driveway. The seven children surrounded the car. They called and begged for the little cat to come to them from under the car. There sat the little cat with children peering at it with big eyes from under the bumpers of the car, and from around all the four wheels. The little cat would not come to all those big eyes.

The little cat sat under the car as saucer-eyed as the saucer-eyed children. It turned its head from side to side, it looked everywhere for some escape, but everywhere were eyes and children. The little cat sat.

When the little cat would not come, the children came. From every side they came crawling flat on their stomachs under the car. At the last moment the little cat tried to scramble away. But a chubby hand reached out and caught it! Backward the boy who had caught the cat crawled from under the car. Backward all seven excited children crawled from under the car. They had a cat!

The seven children ran into the house with the cat. They stormed in a single long row up the stairs to their mother. They all called to their mother up the stairs: "MOTHER, MAY WE HAVE THIS LITTLE CAT? WE FOUND HIM!"

The mother had gone back to bed after dressing the seven children. The alarmed mother sat up in the bed, and looked at the seven children storming into the bedroom. She looked at the little cat. "Now that would be all I would need," she said in dismay. "Seven children and a cat!"

The children gathered around her bed looked at their mother in dismay. Then in the stillness they all heard the woman in the next yard calling "Kitty,

Kitty, Kitty" to her battle-scarred cat. Calling again, "Kitty, Kitty."

"Don't you hear?" the mother in the bed said with a sigh of relief. "The lady next door is calling a cat—so then this must be her cat! Just because you found her cat in our yard does not mean her cat is yours. Now hurry right down, and hurry right over, and take her cat back to her."

"But, Mother!" the biggest boy, who was clutching the cat, said in astonished surprise. "The lady next door has a big black cat. This is a little black cat."

"Yes, Mother," the other six children said hopefully. "A great big cat—not a little black cat!"

"Big cat, black cat—a cat is a cat," the mother said wearily. "And nobody pays much attention to cats—except to their own, maybe. So you don't really know if she has a big black cat or a small black cat. Maybe she has a big cat *and* a small cat. Maybe her big black cat had small black cats. You don't know! So you must quickly take her cat to her—and leave it there with her." And the mother heaved a great sigh of relief, and closed her tired eyes.

In one long row behind their disappointed brother with the little cat, six children clumped down every step of the long stairs. But the littlest girl, coming on behind, said in a big, hopeful whisper down the stairs: "If it isn't the lady's cat, do you suppose Mother will let us keep the little cat?" They all stopped on the stairs.

But from the bed the mother said: "NO—I will not let you keep it. I can't! That would be all I'd need—seven children and a cat!"

Then the seven children clumped down the stairs—every hard wooden step.

The children went silently through their yard, and crawled in a single silent row through the bushes into the yard of the calling woman. The woman turned in alarm to see seven awfully quiet children come into her yard. But her eyes really jumped in alarm when she saw the boy carrying the cat. She looked aghast. "Why, boy!" she said sharply. "That is no way to carry a cat! Is that a way to carry a cat? By its stomach?"

The boy was surprised and taken aback by the woman's sharp words. He nervously squeezed the last little cat. His six brothers and sisters looked from the woman to the squeezed cat. And nobody thought to ask the woman: "Is this your little cat?"

The surprised little boy did not seem to know how to let go his tight hold on the little cat's stomach, except by dropping the cat. He dropped the last little cat at the woman's feet. He backed away from the sharp-voiced woman with his mouth wide open. His three little brothers and three little sisters backed away with their mouths open. It wasn't until they had backed through the bushes into their yard that they closed their mouths and began to play.

In the sixth yard the woman looked at the cat at her feet. But the last little cat looked at the bottom of the big white bowl the woman was holding. It cried up for the milk that it thought was in the bowl. And crying up at the bowl for the milk in the bowl, the little cat's lost voice came back!

The woman looked over the bowl at the crying cat. "Oh, no!" she said. "This isn't for you—this is for my own cat."

But with its new-found voice the little cat kept crying up at the bowl.

"It's meat in the bowl!" the sharp-voiced woman explained to the crying cat. "It's not for you—it's for my Kitty. You're still too little. You should have milk and nothing but milk—but in this bowl is nothing but meat."

She set the bowl down before the little cat to show the last little cat that in the bowl was nothing but long, stringy pieces of raw red meat—and not one drop of milk. The little cat was so hungry it bit into the meat. It tried to drag a long, stringy piece of raw meat out of the bowl.

"You're a thief!" the sharp-voiced woman said. "You mayn't steal my Kitty's meat. To think—you're still so little, but already you're a big thief!"

The little cat went right on dragging the piece of meat over the edge of the bowl. At that moment the woman's big

black warrior cat—lured by the smell of raw red meat—came home. It saw a small black cat dragging a piece of its meat out of its bowl. In one swift silent leap, without a warning or even one yowl, it pounced at the little last cat. But it really pounced on the piece of meat that the little cat was dragging out of the bowl. It was hungry from fighting all night, and it wanted its meat. It did not care about little cats. It cared only about eating red meat, and doing battle with big fighting cats.

But the big black battle-scarred cat looked so mean and so fierce, the last little cat dropped the meat, and scooted away from the bowl. "That's what you get for stealing my Kitty's meat," the sharp-voiced woman called after the little cat. "That's what you get for being a thief!"

The scared little cat did not listen, and did not look back. And even though the big cat was not chasing it, but greedily eating its bowlful of meat, the little scared cat ran straight on. It ran into the yard of the seventh house, up on the porch, and to the back door of the seventh house.

Beyond the seventh house there were no more houses—there was just a field. The big field stretched out from the seventh house, the way the grassy field had stretched out from the kennel-barn. The last little cat did not know, but it was at the last house, on the last porch, at the last door.

Here there was no thick, closed door —the door stood open behind its screen door. But the screen door was closed! The little cat reached up and stood up, and with its new voice it cried into the house through the screen door. But beyond the screen door the whole house was silent and still. There wasn't a sound, there wasn't a motion, and nobody came—there was nobody.

The little cat looked at the porch. On the porch there stood a bowl. The little cat went to the bowl, but in the bowl there was no milk—the bowl was dry and empty. Behind the bowl there lay a bone—an old dry bone some dog had chewed and left there. The little cat sniffed at the bone, but on the bone there was no meat—there wasn't even a smell or a taste of the meat that once had been on the bone. And the little cat sat between a dry bone and a dry bowl, on the porch of the empty last house— at the end of its little cat world.

There was nothing at the last house for the last little cat. Nothing—except the sun! For now the sun came out to take away the cold of the night, and the cold of the gray, slow morning. The sun came out to make the world as warm as a bowlful of milk again. The morning sun shone on the bone and the bowl, and on the little cat. The last little cat was so tired from its long, hard night, the little cat fell asleep in a spot of sun between the bowl and the bone.

The tired little cat had fallen asleep, but the little cat was lost. It was only seven houses and seven yards from the big kennel-barn of the many dogs and the mother cat and the six kittens—but the last little cat was lost. Seven houses and seven yards were all its little cat world. And seven houses and seven yards might just as well have been seven oceans and seven seas and seven prairie plains to a little cat lost. But the lost little cat slept on.

Oh, believe it! A man came to the seventh house, and up on the back porch! The man stopped in surprise at the door of the house to see a little cat asleep on his porch between a bowl and an old dried bone.

"HEY!" said the surprised man to the sleeping cat. "Somebody waiting for me? That's something new, and sort of fine—to come home to find somebody waiting for me!"

The last little cat opened its sleep-bright eyes, and looked up at the man.

The man made fond grumbly sounds in his throat, and picked up the little cat. He picked up the dry, empty bowl. He felt the little cold cat, he felt its flat, empty stomach. In the crook of the man's arm the last little cat began to purr for the man.

"Hey!" said the man. "This is no time to purr! Right now, little cat, you need warmth. Right now, empty cat, you need milk. And after the milk, a long warm sleep, for by the looks of you, you had a terrible night."

With the last little cat in the crook of his arm, the man went into the house, and to the refrigerator in the kitchen. He took out some milk. He started to

pour out some milk into the dry bowl for the little cat, but then he said: "Ah-gah! Icy milk for an icy cat? That will never do. Let's warm the milk!"

He warmed the milk on the kitchen stove. But while he warmed the milk, he held the little cat in the crook of his arm close to the warming stove and the warming milk. The little cat purred for the man, and for the warmth, and for the warming milk. But a hitch and a halt came into its purr—so badly it wanted the milk.

At last the man poured the warm milk into the bowl, and set the bowl down on the floor, and set the little cat down before the bowl. And there it was again at last—in the world!—a bowl of milk! A whole bowl of lovely warm milk!

It was so lovely—the loveliness of lovely warm milk—the little cat dipped its chin and its little black whiskers into the warm white milk. It drank and drank, and lapped and lapped, until its tired tongue could lap no more—and still there was more milk. The little cat had to rest its little tired tongue, but it purred in its throat for the milk—for the man and the milk. And a hitch and a halt came into its purr for the loveliness of the man and his milk.

The man at the kitchen table watched the little cat at the big bowl of milk. At last the little cat came toward the man, for it could hold no more milk. But there was still more milk in the bowl. And the little cat could not quite leave the milk. It sat down halfway between the man and the bowl, purring for the milk and the man, for the man and the milk.

The man laughed fondly at the little cat. And they were together in the quiet house. There wasn't another sound in the house—no other cats, no other dogs.

There was just a warm kitchen, and a quiet man, and a bowl of warm milk. Oh, there was a whole house—a house with rooms, and many things in all the rooms. Later all the things in all the

rooms would have to be looked at by the little cat, and sniffed at, and touched and inspected. Later! Now the little cat wanted to go only as far as the man. Now the little cat at last could leave the milk, and walk to the man. It snuggled itself down on the floor between the feet of the man—as it always had done with the old blind dog.

The man looked down at the little cat cuddled between his feet, and made fond grumbly sounds in his throat. But from looking down at the little cat, the man looked up at the kitchen wall, and at the calendar on the wall. "HEY!" the man said aloud in a big surprise, and pointed to the calendar on the wall. "Hey, it's my birthday, little cat! By the calendar on the wall it's my birthday. I didn't remember and—nobody remembered—it was my birthday. But you came to me on my birthday! Then doesn't that make you my birthday cat? Why, yes! Then you're *my* birthday cat!"

He reached down and scooped up the little cat, and put it in his lap. "Is that a place for a birthday cat—on the floor between my feet?"

The man's lap was so soft and warm, it made the little cat sleepy. The last little cat purred a sleepy song for the man and his milk, for the man and his lap—for the good man and his good lap.

But the man jumped up, and set the little cat down again. "I just now thought of it," said the excited man. "But if you are now my birthday cat— why, then, shouldn't you have a birthday present on my birthday, little cat?" He picked up the little cat again, and excitedly set it down before the bowl with milk. "Don't you worry and don't you fret," he told the little cat. "Just sit beside your bowl of milk while

I go to get your birthday present. I won't be gone long—it's just a run and a dash across seven yards."

The man ran out of the door. The little cat sat beside the bowl of milk where he had placed it. Oh, once it went into another room, and once it started to go down to the basement—to look at all the things in the room and all the things in the basement. But it rushed right back to its bowl of milk, to see if it still was there—and to sing a song for the bowl of milk, because it still was there. Sing a purry song for the loveliness of lovely milk, and a bowlful of milk all its own—in a house all its own!

In almost no time the man was back, for the man had simply run across the seven back yards behind the seven houses to the big kennel-barn. Believe it—for this was the man who owned the kennel-barn, and took care of all the dogs.

The kennel-barn stood at one end of the row of seven houses; the man lived in the seventh house at the other end of the row of houses. And to the man the seven yards were hardly more than seventy-seven and eleven big steps. And seventy-seven and eleven long, running steps back. While to the last little cat, lost in the night, seven houses and seven yards might just as well have been seven oceans and seven seas and seven prairie plains.

The man did not come back alone. The man came back with a wire cage. Oh, believe it! Inside the cage was the old blind dog!

The man set the cage down on the floor before the last little cat. "This you may think queer," the man said to the little cat. "A dog as a present for a cat!

But this I thought should be your birthday present on *my* birthday."

"Now that you live here in this house —and you will live here!—I won't need to keep my poor old dog in all that noise and din of dogs in the kennel-barn. All my old dog still wants is a little peace and a little quiet, and a little milk, and a little company, and a lot of sleep. But with me at work, my poor old dog would get so lonely in the house—I had to keep him in the kennel-barn. But with you in the house —oh, I hope you two can get along together—my old blind dog should not be lonely any more. And he'll have peace and quiet and company, and a bowl of milk, and a lot of sleep."

Then after making his big hopeful birthday speech, the man opened the door of the wire cage to let the dog out

to show the blind dog to the little cat. But to the man's surprise, the little cat walked into the cage to the old blind dog. And when the blind dog felt his little cat, the dog made nice old noises in his throat, stretched out his paws, and stretched down to the little cat. And the little cat walked in between the paws of the old blind dog, and tucked itself in under his woolly chin. The little cat purred, and the dog made nice fond noises in his throat.

But the man stood shaking and shaking his surprised head. He had not known about the last little cat living with the old blind dog in the wire cage in the kennel-barn—he did not understand it at all.

But one thing he knew—it was marvelous! Oh, believe it—it was marvelous. It was three times, four times marvelous in the seventh and last house.

The last little cat had become a birthday cat, and though it had no birthday of its own, it had a birthday

present all its own. The old blind dog!

And the old blind dog had the little cat. And they both had a man and a

house for their own. A good man, and a
whole house! They were home!

The last little cat at last was home.

MEINDERT DEJONG WAS BORN IN THE VILLAGE OF Weirum in The Netherlands. When he was eight years old his family moved to Grand Rapids, Michigan, where he lived ever since.

Winner of the 1954 Newbery Award for *The Wheel On The School*. Mr. DeJong has written many books for children. Of one of his books the New York *Herald Tribune* said, "Few writers of today offer this sort of realism to the young, with its insight that stimulates the imagination and its clear beauty."

Meindert DeJong was educated at religious schools maintained by the Dutch Calvinists, and received his B.A. degree from Calvin College. He also studied at the University of Chicago.

Whole Spirit Press specializes in reissuing out-of-print books that help the reader learn from the inside out. We also work with authors that have a specific passion they wish to share with children. If you wish to learn more about our publications, please visit us at wholespiritpress.com.

Many of our publications are designed to complement a lesson taught in a specific grade. Our newest venture of early readers is designed to enhance the opportunities for our children to become better readers and, at the same time create a love of nature and the environment.

Title	Grade
Early Readers- 6 books	1st -3rd
The Secret Pet (Sequel to Early Readers)	2nd-3rd
The Last Little Cat by Meindert DeJong	2nd-4th
Sticks Across the Chimney: A Story of Denmark by Nora Burglon	4th
The Gate Swings In: A Story of Sweden by Nora Burglon	4th
Gilgamesh: Man's First Story By Bernarda Bryson	5th
The Boy Apprenticed to an Enchanter By Padraic Colum	6th-7th
String, Straightedge and Shadow The Story of Geometry By Julia Diggins	6th-7th
Making Math Meaningful Series Curriculum, Teacher's and Student Workbooks By Jamie York	6th-8th
Making Math Meaningful: Fun with Puzzles Games and More by Jamie York	$6^{th} - 12^{th}$
Making Math Meaningful: Sourcebook for 1st-5th Teaching Grades One Through Five	

Please check our website or call for current pricing and shipping options.

Whole Spirit Press
1905 S. Clarkson St.
Denver, CO 80210
http://wholespiritpress.com
Phone: 1-877-488-3774
Fax: 303-979-6151